For Pete and Shirley Davies, with all my love x
~ S. M.

For Mom, Dad, and Rachel
~ C. G.

tiger tales
5 River Road, Suite 128, Wilton, CT 06897
Published in the United States 2020
Originally published in Great Britain 2020
by Little Tiger Press Ltd.
Text by S. Marendaz
Illustrations by Carly Gledhill
Text and illustrations copyright © 2020 Little Tiger Press Ltd.
ISBN-13: 978-1-68010-186-7
ISBN-10: 1-68010-186-2
Printed in China
LTP/1800/2900/0819

For more insight and activities, visit us at www.tigertalesbooks.com

THE BEDTIME BOOK

by

S. MARENDAZ

Illustrated by

CARLY GLEDHILL

tiger tales

It was a cool, still night, and Frank was cuddled up in bed.

He closed his eyes.
He snuggled under his blanket.
He was just about to fall asleep when . . .

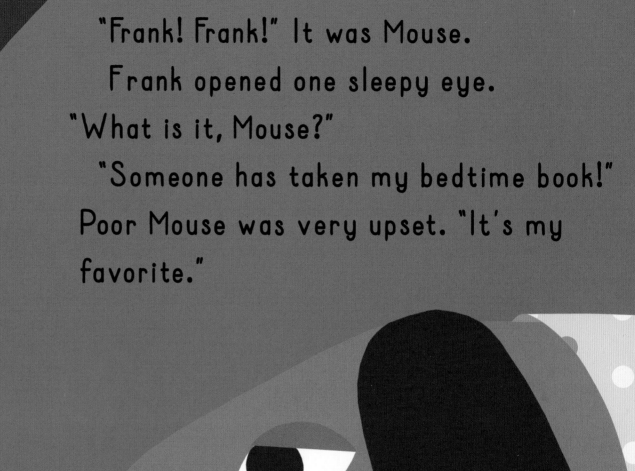

"Frank! Frank!" It was Mouse.
Frank opened one sleepy eye.
"What is it, Mouse?"
"Someone has taken my bedtime book!"
Poor Mouse was very upset. "It's my
favorite."

"Oh, dear," said Frank. "Maybe your book is just hiding somewhere."

"But I put it outside my flowerpot," squeaked Mouse. "And when I went home, it was GONE."

Frank went with Mouse
to her flowerpot.

Scurry,

scurry,

scurry.

Pant,

pant,

pant.

Just as Mouse said,
there was no book outside.

"Your book IS gone,"
agreed Frank.

"But what's this?" sniffed Frank.
Sniff . . . sniff . . . "It's a trail!"
Sniff!
Sniff!
Sniff!

Frank and Mouse followed the trail up
... down ... and around, until at last
it led them to ...

"Bella! Did you take Mouse's book?" asked Frank.

"Hmm," said Bella. "Did it have a blue cover?"
"Yes! Yes! That's my book!" Mouse was very excited.
"Oh," said Bella. "I thought it was a lost book!
I put it by the flowers where Owl lives."

"Quick! We'll find it, Mouse!"
cried Frank.
They all rushed over to Owl's house.

Scurry,

scurry,

scurry.

Pant,
pant,
pant.

But when they got there,
they didn't see Mouse's book.

They looked high.

And they looked low.

But they couldn't find
Mouse's book anywhere.

"My book is lost forever!"
cried Mouse. She was very upset.

Bella and Frank patted
Mouse's back kindly.

"Book?" asked a voice.
It was Owl. "I found a
book! Does it have shiny
stars on the cover?"

"Yes! Yes! That's my book!" said Mouse.
"Oh, dear," said Owl. "I took it to
Baby Hedgehog. I thought he would like
a bedtime story."

"Quick! We'll get it, Mouse!" cried Frank.

But Mouse shook her head. "I can't take it back from Baby Hedgehog. The book will make him very happy."
She walked sadly away to bed.

Back in his bed, Frank snuggled his nose under the blanket.
He closed his eyes.
But he couldn't sleep.
"Mouse will be sad without her favorite book," sighed Frank. "She was so kind to share it with Baby Hedgehog."

Suddenly, Frank had a wonderful idea.

He rushed over to
Mouse's flowerpot.

Pant,

pant,

pant.

"Mouse! Mouse! Are you awake?"

"I brought you my favorite bedtime book, Mouse,"
said Frank. "I thought we could read it together."
Mouse was very happy. The two friends settled
down, and Frank started reading.

The story sounded familiar.

Mouse looked at the front cover.
It was blue, with shiny stars.

"Frank! That's MY book! We have
the same favorite book!"

"We DO? How about that!"

So Mouse and Frank read their favorite book
all the way to the end . . . . .
And together they fell fast asleep
under the starry sky.

Snore,

snore,

snore.